THE ROMAN TWINS

ROY GERRARD

Farrar Straus Giroux • New York

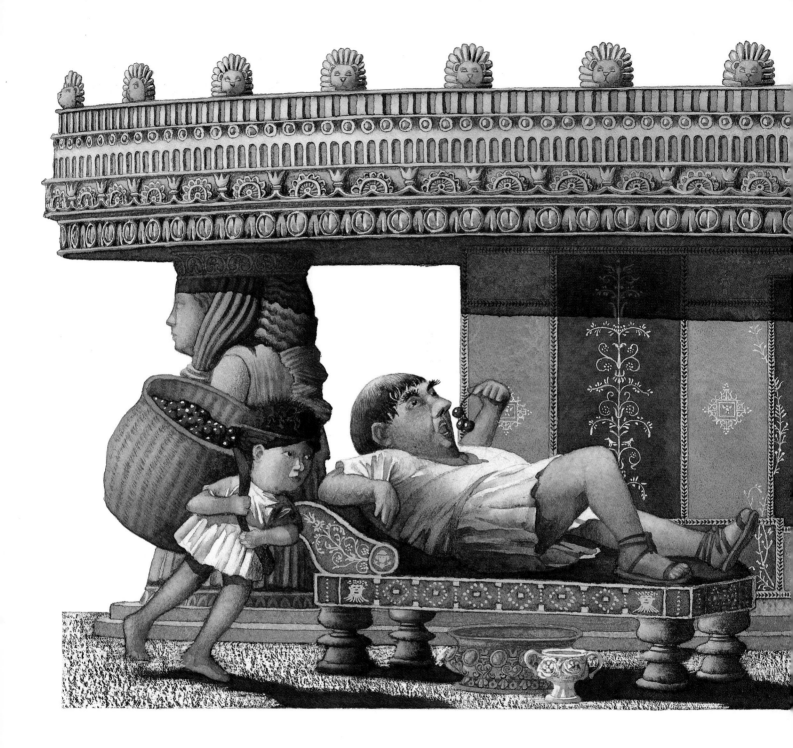

Young Maximus, though just a boy, was doomed to be a slave
And serve a cruel master from the cradle to the grave.
Although he worked from dawn till dusk, no matter how he tried,
His owner, Slobbus Pompius, was never satisfied.

Vanilla, his twin sister, worked for Lady Pompius,
A proud and haughty woman who created such a fuss
If pots and pans weren't gleaming or her hair was not done right
That poor Vanilla crawled to bed exhausted every night.

The slaves were always given heaps of heavy work to do,
And when one job was finished, Slobbus thought of something new.
The task which they most hated and which really wore them down
Was carrying the litter when their owners went to town.

Then Maxi and Vanilla had to trudge with aching feet
Along the hot and dusty road and down the cobbled street;
Not daring to complain, nonetheless the pair felt bitter,
Forced to fetch and cart around two fatties on a litter.

They left their lazy master at the public baths each day,
Where he would gorge and gossip, just to pass the time away.
The slaves, meanwhile, pressed on, never tarrying or stopping,
Carrying their mistress on an endless round of shopping.

The streets were very stony and the youngsters' feet would bleed
When Lady P. went bargaining for things she didn't need.
Then back they'd go for Slobbus, to continue their ordeal
By tottering off home again to make the evening meal.

Now, one day Slobbus went to buy a chariot and horse,

Imagining the neighbors would be most impressed, of course,

To see him and his lady gaily galloping around,

But horses can be difficult, as Slobbus quickly found.

Though Polydox, the trusty steed, was gentle with each slave,
When Slobbus Pompius approached, he'd snort and misbehave.
Then Slobbus, in a rage at this embarrassing defeat,
Decided he would slay the nag and chop him up for meat.

Vanilla and her brother pleaded for the creature's life,
But Slobbus would not change his mind, and neither would his wife.
So out into the field that night the daring twosome crept
And stole away with Polydox, while nasty Slobbus slept.

Next morning when their master found their cold and empty beds,
He flew into a temper and declared he'd have their heads,
And Lady Pompius went wild and said it wasn't fair,
Who was there now to clean her house and tidy up her hair?

Slobbus asked his cousin, who was captain of the legion,
To send his men forthwith on a search throughout the region.
The captain told them boastfully that once he'd caught the slaves,
He'd spare their lives just long enough to make them dig their graves.

So up and down the soldiers searched the town till darkness fell,
But where their prey was hidden, it seemed nobody could tell.
The troops grew lackadaisical and soon marched home for tea;
The captain of the legion was disgruntled as could be.

Then Slobbus was beside himself with anger and despair,
With nobody to wait on him and comb his lady's hair.
He swore he'd find the fugitives, and with their lives they'd pay.
His victims, in the interim, had safely snuck away.

For now the slaves and Polydux were snugly bedded down,
Well hidden in a stable in the humblest part of town.
Their host was named Spontanius, and though he risked his life,
He chose to help his friends, and so did Chubbia, his wife.

Spontanius and Chubbia sold kindling in the street,
But being very poor, they barely had enough to eat,
And Maxi and Vanilla, although welcome to their share,
Were fed for doing nothing, and they felt it wasn't fair.

They knew they were a burden, till they heard Spontanius say
The Emperor would hold the annual chariot race next day.
At this, the twins, who'd thought of maybe giving themselves up,
Agreed instead to enter for the Emperor's Gold Cup.

Knowing well that Polydox would not obey a stranger,
They took the reins themselves, disregarding any danger.
By luck, the rule for racing was that everybody must
Tie on a kerchief round the face to keep away the dust.

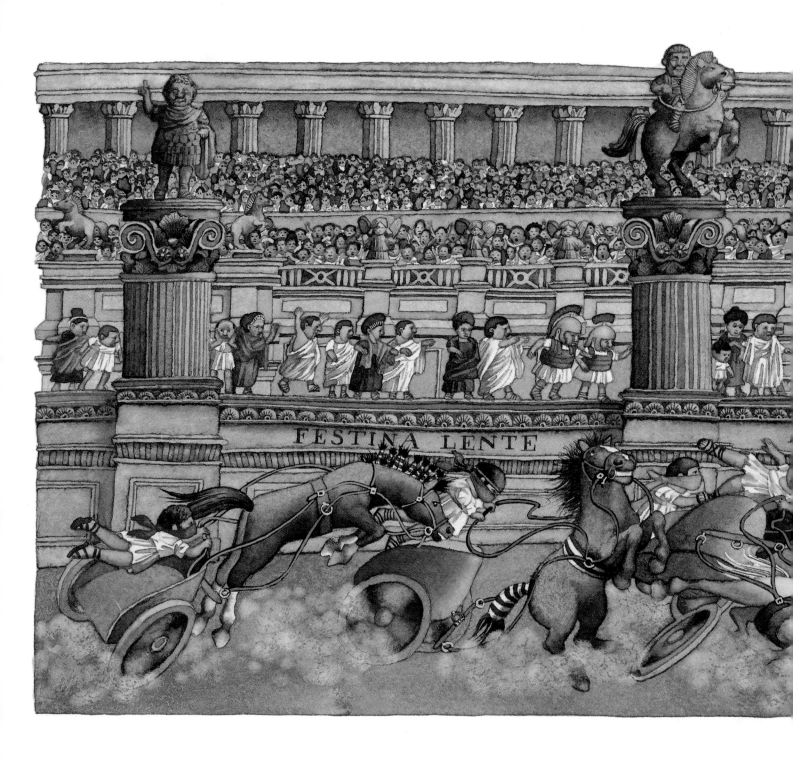

Now, once the race began, before the vast and cheering crowd,
Their horse's speed and daring made the pair of them feel proud.
Vanilla and her brother were elated and surprised,
For Polydox was swifter than they'd ever realized.

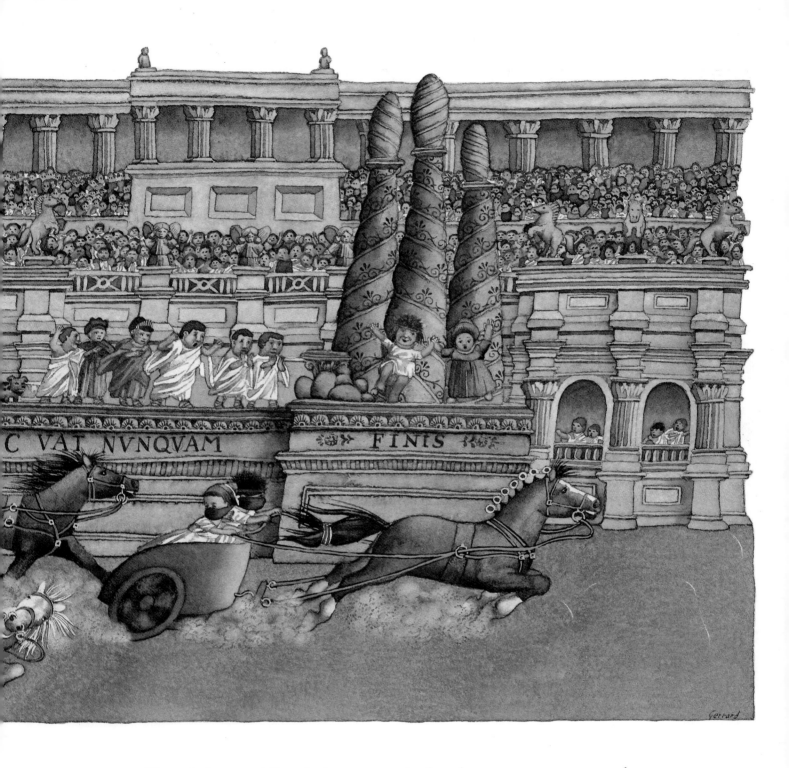

Though horses fell and chariots crashed and some were overturned,
In spite of all the rumpus Polydox seemed unconcerned.
Around the wrecks he nimbly swerved while never losing speed,
And when they reached the finish, Polydox was in the lead!

When taken to the palace to receive the winner's prize,
They entered with their kerchiefs off, no longer in disguise.
And wouldn't you just know it, Slobbus Pompius was there
To claim revenge against them, for he'd recognized the pair.

The Emperor was in a fix and wondered what to do.
The law demanded runaways should suffer death, it's true,
And yet he felt the common folk would think it a disgrace
To punish plucky children who had triumphed in the race.

But as the people waited for the Emperor to choose,
A messenger came bursting in and brought alarming news—
The Ostrogoths were coming, that most fierce and savage band
Whose bad behavior caused a wave of panic in the land.

And where were all the soldiers who would drive the Goths away?
The Roman army, to a man, had gone on holiday!
The hordes could cross the Tiber bridge, and if they were annoyed,
They'd burn the whole of Rome, therefore the bridge must be destroyed.

Then out spoke bold Spontanius and gave the people hope
By pointing out that as the bridge was only held with rope,
If some brave souls would volunteer to cut those ropes away,
He'd guard them as they worked and also keep the Goths at bay.

Then Chubbia spoke up—her voice was quivering with pride—
And said if he faced danger, she must be there by his side.
And Maxi and Vanilla said that they would help him, too,
But barely had they started when the Goths came into view.

The Ostrogoths all laughed to see Spontanius alone;
It tickled them to think one man would face them on his own.
He wasn't much to look at, but it must be understood,
His arms were strong and muscular from chopping all that wood.

First Wulfus the Unwashed One, who was leader of the pack,
With sword in hand and sneer on face, advanced to the attack.
But when the Goths saw Wulfus flattened with a single blow,
No other from that army was prepared to have a go.

The ropes behind Spontanius were quickly cut away;
His friends, meanwhile, retreated as the bridge began to sway.
Then, with the broken bridge behind and Ostrogoths before,
He dived into the river and swam strongly for the shore.

And when at last Spontanius stood firmly on dry ground,
The citizens rejoiced to see their hero safe and sound.
The Emperor saluted them and issued a decree:
The slaves were given Polydox and both of them set free!

To show the four his gratitude, he gave them gifts of gold,
But seeing Slobbus was still vexed, his look grew stern and cold.
Then white with rage at hearing the ungrateful wretch complain,
He ordered Slobbus—by himself!—to build the bridge again.

Triumphantly the famous four paraded through the streets,
And then a feast was held for them with lots of tasty treats.
The party was attended by just everyone in Rome
(Except for Slobbus and his wife, who sulked and stayed at home).

When all the fun and games were done, there's little more to tell,
Considering the hazards, things had turned out rather well.
So Polydox and Maximus, Vanilla and their friends
Gained freedom, wealth, and glory, and that's where the story ends.

Copyright © 1998 by Roy Gerrard
All rights reserved
First published in Great Britain by Hamish Hamilton, Ltd.
Printed and bound in Singapore by IMAGO
First American edition, 1998

Library of Congress Cataloging-in-Publication Data
Gerrard, Roy.
    The Roman twins / Roy Gerrard. — 1st American ed.
        p.   cm.
    Summary: Maximus and his twin sister Vanilla, slaves to the cruel and greedy Slobbus Pompius,
risk their lives to save a horse and end up helping to save the city of Rome from the Goths.
    ISBN 0-374-36339-0
    [1. Rome—Fiction. 2. Slavery—Rome—Fiction. 3. Stories in rhyme.] I. Title.
PZ8.3.G323Rm   1998
[Fic]—DC21   97-42163